LUIGI'S ALL·NIGHT CAR PARK

Joshua Schreier

ABC
London

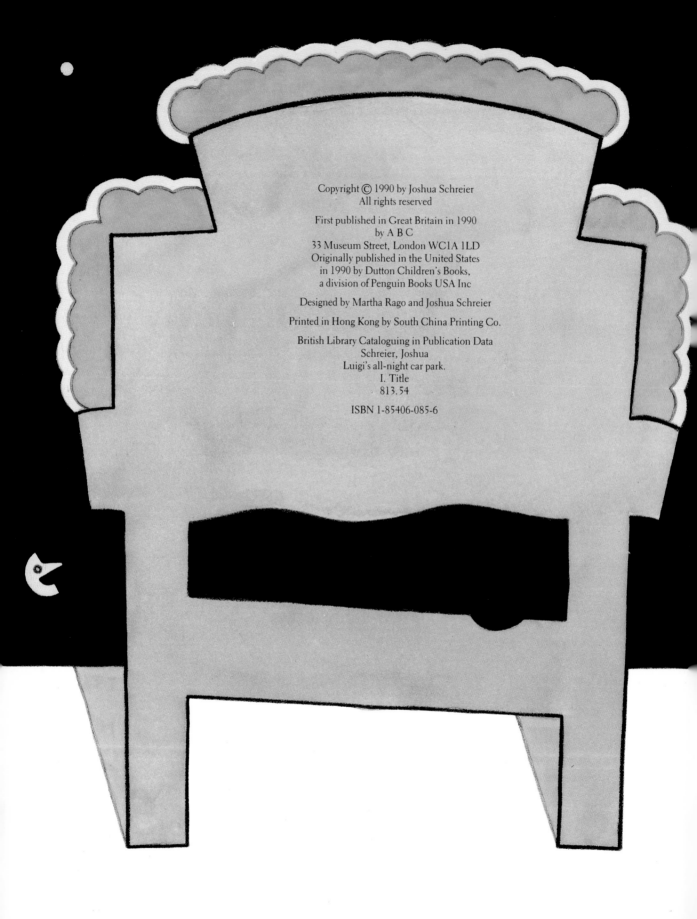

First published in Great Britain in 1990
by A B C
33 Museum Street, London WC1A 1LD
Originally published in the United States
in 1990 by Dutton Children's Books,
a division of Penguin Books USA Inc

Designed by Martha Rago and Joshua Schreier

Printed in Hong Kong by South China Printing Co.

British Library Cataloguing in Publication Data
Schreier, Joshua
Luigi's all-night car park.
I. Title
813.54

ISBN 1-85406-085-6

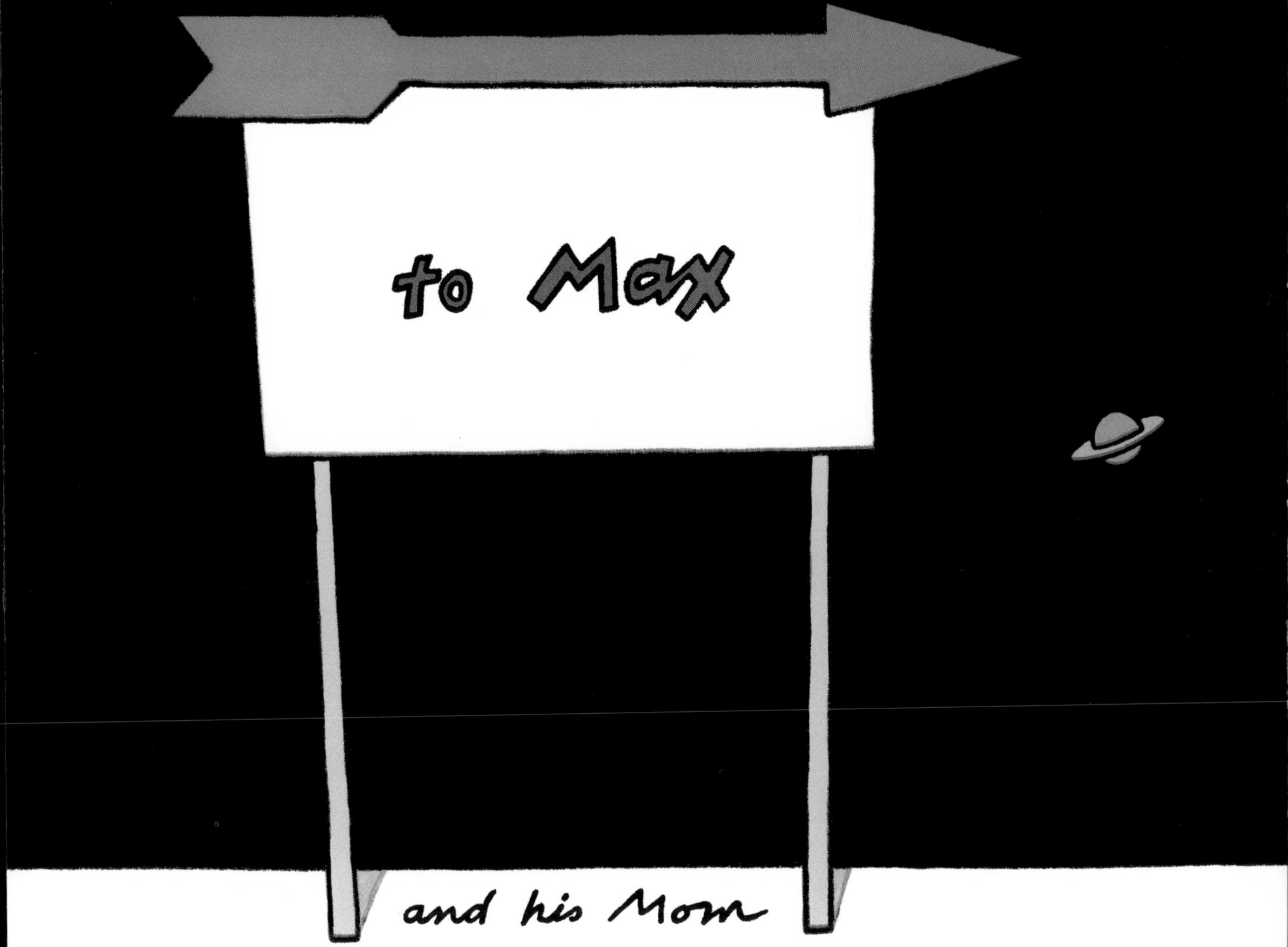
to Max
and his Mom

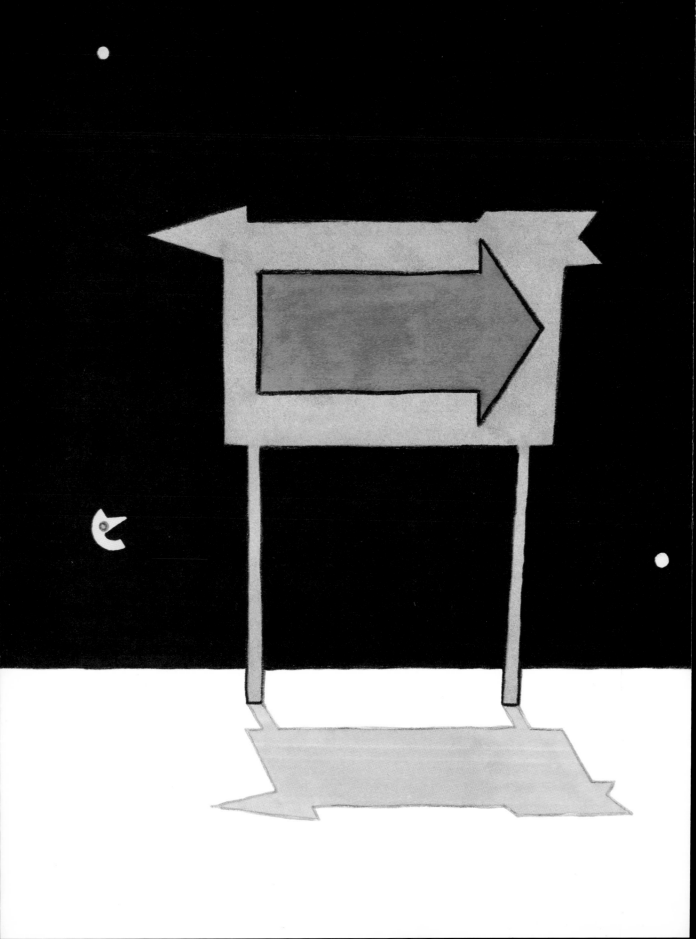

Welcome to Luigi's. We're open all night. We park cars—and other things. Nothing is too big or too small. We're empty now—but wait.

If it stops and goes, it's welcome at Luigi's. Even a bus. No queues, no waiting. Just drive in.

Hello, Oliver Fenderbender. You're a regular customer. Mind the bus! What about that spot? No? Well, drive around and find a place you like. And behave yourself!

Hello, Purplefellow. How did you fit into that little car? Don't forget your parking ticket.

Brooom, Vrooom! Still haven't found your parking places? Then keep driving, everybody. Drive straight in, Jeepster Robot. Do your batteries need charging?

Beep! Beep! Look out, Oliver! BANG! CRASH! Oh, no, not again! Oliver Fenderbender, how many times do I have to tell you? Be careful.

Is that you, Rosa? Want to park your boat? No problem—row straight in.

Heads down! Here comes a helicopter.
WHOOPA-WHOOPA-WHOOPA. We're
busy tonight. Keep moving, everybody.

I'm hungry. Time for a snack. Want a grape,
Oliver? Or are you too busy changing your tyre?
    What about you, Rosa, Jeepster Robot,
Purplefellow? Say thank you.
    Make room for the helicopter, Rosa. Good
evening, Red Racingcar. No speeding!

Chuffa-chuffa-chuffa-woo-WOOooo. Here comes train number 524! At Luigi's, we park anything—even if it takes up three spaces.

Good evening, Greycar. Nice to see you tonight. Funny—nobody has found a parking space yet. Well, just keep moving. Look! Up in the sky…

RRRRRRRRRrrrrrrrrrmmmmmmmmmm.
Watch out! Here comes a flying saucer!

Luigi! Time to clear up. It's getting late.
But, Dad, my car park's open all night.
No buts, Luigi. It's time for bed.
Just two more minutes, Dad...please?
All right, Luigi.

At last. Everyone's just about parked. Just as well, because Luigi's All-Night Car Park is about to close. I'm tired.

Good night, Oliver. Good night, Rosa, Jeepster Robot, Red Racingcar. Good night, Purplefellow. Good night, Greycar.

Good night, Dad.
Good night, Luigi.